GORMY RUCKLES
Monster Birthday

GUY BASS
Illustrations by Ross Collins

SCHOLASTIC

Look out for other monster adventures:

Meet the Ruckles

(If You Dare)

Gormy Ruckles, the monster boy, was very small, very blue and very hairy. He had a long tail and just one quite good fang. Gormy lived at No. 1 Peatree Hill with his mother, Mogra the Horrid, and his father, Grumbor the Grim.

If you ever happen to run into them. . .

. . .keep running!

To Joseph, Freddie and Emily
Three little monsters!

First published in the UK in 2009 by Scholastic Children's Books
An imprint of Scholastic Ltd
Euston House, 24 Eversholt Street
London, NW1 1DB, UK
Registered office: Westfield Road, Southam, Warwickshire, CV47 0RA
SCHOLASTIC and associated logos are trademarks and/or registered
trademarks of Scholastic Inc.

ISBN 978 1 407 10850 6

A CIP catalogue record for this book
is available from the British Library

Printed in the UK by CPI Bookmarque, Croydon
Papers used by Scholastic Children's Books are made
from wood grown in sustainable forests.

1 3 5 7 9 10 8 6 4 2

www.scholastic.co.uk/zone

OnE

Happy (one eighth-and-an eighth) Birthday!

Gormy woke up just as the sun began to peek over Peatree Hill. It was the forty-second time he had woken up that night. Then again, he was surprised he had got any sleep at all – today was Gormy's birthday! And not just any birthday – today, Gormy Ruckles was turning *one-*

1

eighth-and-an-eighth. As far as he was concerned, being one-eighth-and-an-eighth meant he was finally a *real monster*.

I wonder what I look like now I'm a real monster? Gormy thought, sitting up in bed. *I must be at least as big as my dad. No, bigger! I bet I have a hundred horns on my head, and tusks as thick as tree trunks. Or claws that drag along the ground!* He couldn't wait to find out. He leapt out of bed and delved into his Big Chest of Monstrously Excellent things. He rummaged past a smashing bone and a packet of dried snack-rats and took out a large, silver plate. As monsters don't have mirrors (most monsters look far too scary to risk looking at their own reflection), Gormy had spent two days polishing the plate so that he would be able to see exactly how monstrous he looked on his birthday. Gormy held the plate in front of his face and stared at it. Oddly, he couldn't see a hundred horns. He couldn't make out any tusks or claws either, for that matter.

Maybe I didn't polish the plate hard enough, thought Gormy. He decided to go downstairs and check how he looked in one of the shiny saucepans. He rushed out of his room and bounced down the massive stairs. But as he was racing towards the kitchen. . .

DOMP!

Gormy bumped into his father! He looked up and saw Grumbor towering above him. He was a huge, terrifying monster, with twice as many teeth, tusks and horns than were practical. He had won the *Monster of Monsters Most Stomped Village Award* two years running, and had once roared an entire herd of cows to death.

"I was just coming to find you," said Grumbor, in a voice that sounded like fifty rocks being hit with fifty hammers. "So how does it feel to be one-eighth-and-an-eighth?"

"Small," muttered Gormy, wondering why he was still tinier than one of his father's toeclaws. He ran into the kitchen to find his mother, Mogra, making breakfast. She was just as big as ever too! Which was about as big as a garden shed, but much more hairy and pink.

"Happy birthday, Gormy! I'm just rolling some puppy pancakes. How about a glass of goatshake while you wait? I shook the goat fresh this morning," she said.

"What's going on? Why are you both still big? I mean, why am I still small? I'm one-eighth-and-an-eighth!" said Gormy in desperation. Grumbor laughed so hard that cracks appeared in the walls.

"It takes more than one birthday to

make you a monster," he said. "What did you think, that you'd just wake up and be as big as me?"

"Well, I . . . no," lied Gormy, suddenly a bit embarrassed.

"Oh Gormy, you don't just change into a monster overnight. It takes *years*. You shouldn't be so impatient to grow up," said Mogra, handing him a pancake. "Here, I've put an extra puppy in it for you."

"Thanks," said Gormy, meekly. He couldn't believe how stupid he'd been. This was turning out to be the worst birthday *ever*! Even worse than the one where he lost his milk fang in his birthday cake! He slumped to the floor, feeling like the whole day was ruined.

"You should eat up," said Grumbor, swallowing five pancakes at once. "You'll

need all your strength in the land beyond
the hill."

"*The land beyond the hill?*" Gormy
repeated, his furry blue lip quivering with
excitement.

"Oh, did I forget to mention it?" said
Grumbor with a monstrous grin. "We're
going *fishing*."

TWO

How To Catch a Fish
(with a rock)

Gormy couldn't believe it! He was going to the land beyond the hill for the first time ever (that is, apart from the time he had to go and rescue his sheep from a pack of wolves, but as that was a *very big secret*, it didn't really count). And what's more, he was going fishing!

Gormy had never even seen a fish before, never mind eaten one. Monsters always talked about fish in hushed, nervous tones, but Gormy had never thought to ask why. It certainly wasn't one of the sixteen questions he asked his father in a single breath.

"When are we going? Can we go now? Can Mike come too? Will I see any hoomums? Will we see a hundred hoomums? Will we see a *million*? How many is a million? When are we going? Where do we catch the fish? How do we catch the fish? How many fish will we catch? What does a fish look like? What *is* a fish? Is it like a bird? Does it have wings? When are we going?"

"Finish your breakfast," said Grumbor. "Monsters never go anywhere on an empty stomach. Then fetch your **How to be a Better Monster** book and meet me at the front door."

Gormy swallowed his breakfast without a single chew, burped politely, then ran up to his room. He got out his backpack and put his **How to be a Better Monster** book (which contained all six hundred and eleventy-six of his monstering lessons)

inside, then rushed downstairs
and out of the front door.

"Many happy returns,
Gormy!" came a small, gruff
voice. There, perched on a
hanging basket (of stinging
nettles – it was a
monstrous house, after
all) was Mike the
scuttybug. Mike was
Gormy's only friend,
and despite being ugly,
slimy and smelly, he was the
best friend a monster boy could ask for.

"Mike! You won't believe it – I'm going
to the land beyond the hill!" squealed
Gormy.

"Great! Plenty of fresh, tasty dung in
the land beyond the hill," Mike replied,

getting that glazed look he always got when he thought about his favourite food. "Mind if I tag along?" he added, scuttying inside Gormy's backpack.

"Right, it's time we were off," said Grumbor, emerging from behind the house with a truly enormous sack of rocks on his back.

"What are the rocks for?" asked Gormy.

"Fishing, of course," said Grumbor. "Can't fish without rocks."

Now more excited than ever, Gormy followed his father down Peatree Hill. They worked their way through the thick ring of trees that surrounded the hill and made it look, from the outside, like a scary forest. Finally, they reached the edge. Grumbor pushed a tree aside with his vast claws.

"What are you waiting for?" said Grumbor. Gormy took a deep breath into three of his four lungs, and clambered through.

He was in the land beyond the hill.

It was even more mind-boggling than Gormy remembered! In fact, it was probably the most boggled his mind had ever been. He stared out across the endless valley. It was impossible to see it all. There was every colour, shape and smell Gormy could imagine. Cows and sheep grazed lazily in lush, green fields, which spread out as far as the eye could see. Tall trees cast long shadows in the morning sun, and a warm, welcoming breeze brushed across Gormy's fur.

Then, as his eyes darted in every direction, Gormy noticed something else. It was a hoomum village. He had never seen one so close-up before! There were small, wooden houses with thatched roofs, and more hoomums than he could count. They

looked even stranger than he remembered – almost hairless, and covered in "cloves" to try and make themselves look less edible.

"Can I scare some hoomums?" he asked, with a monstrous glint in his eye.

"Absolutely not," said Grumbor. "You must *never* approach hoomums in the day. There are just too many of them. If they can see you coming, they'll have time to get together and attack *you*! That's why I usually only monster at night."

Gormy sighed. At this rate he was never going to scare a hoomum! Being one-eighth-and-an-eighth wasn't turning out at all like he had hoped.

"Don't worry, there's plenty of monstrousness to come – we're nearly at the river," said Grumbor as he wandered down the hill. Gormy scampered after him.

The river cut through the valley like a giant, endless snake, and beneath its silvery surface, Gormy could see dozens of brightly-coloured creatures darting around as if they were late for something.

"What *are* they?" asked Gormy, peering into the water.

"They're what we came for! They're *fish*, and you can't go fishing without fish," chuckled Grumbor, taking an enormous rock out of the bag. "Now, watch and learn."

"This should be good," said Mike, poking his greasy head out of Gormy's backpack. Gormy and Mike watched Grumbor lift the rock high above his head. He waited for the right moment, took aim, and threw!

BOOOOSH!

Water and fish went everywhere! They

scattered in their dozens along the banks of the river, flipping and flapping in horrid bewilderment. One even bounced off Gormy's head!

"Can I have a go?" squealed Gormy, jumping up and down. Grumbor poured the sack of rocks out on to the ground. Gormy grabbed the biggest one that he could lift, and waited for the fishiest fish that he could see. He took aim, and threw!

PLISH!

"I got him!" cried Gormy. Sure enough, a small, stunned fish bobbed to the surface of the water. It didn't look at all like he thought it would (it didn't have wings or a beak or anything). It didn't even look very tasty, not like a hoomum. Still, he *was* a monster, so the least he could do was eat it. He was just about to pop it in his mouth when. . .

"*Don't eat that!*" yelled Grumbor. His voice was so thunderous that it caused a small earthquake in the next valley.

"That's a fish! Monsters can't eat fish! In fact, it's the only thing we cannot eat. Cows, sheep, hoomums, rocks – they're all fine – but not fish!"

"What happens if monsters eat fish?" said Gormy. He saw his father shudder, for the first time ever. Then Grumbor shook his head, and spoke a single word.

"*Croodles.*"

Three

Croodles

"What's Croodles?" asked Gormy, nervously.

"Croodles is the worst thing a monster can suffer – a bellyache of monstrous proportions," replied Grumbor. "*Anything* can happen with a bout of Croodles. Absolutely anything! It is the one single advantage that hoomums have over monsters. Hoomums can eat fish. In fact, they love it! But we monsters cannot."

"I bet *you* could eat a fish, Dad," Gormy said.

"I tried, once. I was on a fishing trip, just like you. My father warned me not to eat it, but I wouldn't listen. I wolfed that fish down in one gulp. I thought I was the most monstrous monster in the whole world. But then, the Croodles began."

"What happened?" asked a wide-eyed Gormy.

"Let's just say it was the longest day of my life! There was nothing I could do except wait for the fish to . . . come out the other end. Lesson six hundred and eleventy-seven: Monsters Can't Eat Fish. Not even me."

"Then, why do we throw rocks at them?" asked Gormy.

"Why? Because it's monstrous!" said Grumbor. Suddenly, he grabbed a rock and stomped down the riverbank, shouting, "Look, there's another one!"

Gormy stared at the fish in his paws. He couldn't believe something so small and unmonstrous could cause so much trouble.

"I bet *I* wouldn't get Croodles," he whispered, as Mike scuttied around his head. "Not now I'm one eighth-and-an-eighth."

"You're not thinking about what I think you're thinking about, are you?" said Mike, right into Gormy's ear, "because that

Croodles sounds like a whole mess of trouble. If you're hungry, why don't I roll you a nice ball of dung?"

But it was too late. Gormy shoved the fish into his mouth and swallowed it whole!

 He waited a moment, half expecting his guts to explode . . . but nothing happened. Not so much as a belly-twinge. Gormy couldn't believe he'd done it! He hadn't even got a *touch* of Croodles!

"I did it!" Gormy squealed. He immediately raced after his father, shouting, "Dad, Dad! I did it, I—" but he suddenly stopped. He couldn't tell his father that he'd disobeyed him on their first trip out. He'd never be allowed to leave Peatree Hill again!

"What is it? What did you do?" Grumbor asked, spinning around. His rock flew out of his hand, squashing a passing sheep.

"I . . . I did . . . nothing," muttered Gormy.

Grumbor shook his head. "Nothing? Why would you shout about doing nothing? Honestly, here I am trying to teach you how to be monstrous, and you're not even paying attention," Grumbor sighed, and began tramping back up the hill (picking up the squashed sheep on the way – he hated to waste food).

Meanwhile, Gormy couldn't believe what he'd done. He tried not to grin, but it was no good. He had to cover his mouth with both paws so that Grumbor didn't see.

Four

Surprise!

By the time Gormy and his father got back to the hill, Gormy had decided that turning one-eighth-and-an-eighth was the best thing that had ever happened to him. He had turned into the most monstrous monster ever! He could even eat fish without getting Croodles! As he swung the front door open, Gormy was sure the day couldn't get any better.

"Surprise!" cried his mother. She'd thrown a party for him! Well, sort of. Gormy didn't have enough friends for an actual party. Also, Mike (who was understandably wary of being stepped on) had already scuttied off. But it was still very exciting. There was a banner strung across the ceiling that read "Happy Birthday Gormy" and Mogra was holding the biggest sack of presents Gormy had ever seen!

"Here you go, Gormy – many happy returns!" said his mother, handing him the sack. Gormy rummaged through it with glee. Inside he found:

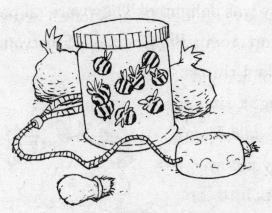

🐾 ONE LUCKY RABBIT'S FOOT

(to go with Gormy's lucky goat's nose

and lucky cow's head)

🐾 TWO BAGS OF BOMB-SWEETS

(you never know whether

you'll get a sweet or a bomb. . .)

🐾 ONE JAR OF ANGRY BEES

(for eating, playing or writing with)

ONE ENDLESS SOAP-ON-A-ROPE

(a never-ending soap bar for keeping
monstrous fur clean and glossy).

Gormy was delighted! They were all perfect
additions to his Big Chest of Monstrously
Excellent things.

"Right, time for
cake," said Mogra.
Gormy followed his
parents into the
kitchen. There,
on the table, was
the biggest
birthday cake he'd
ever seen. It was
at least eight
times bigger
than he was,

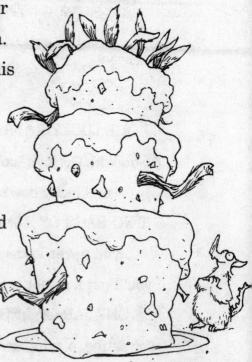

and made from all his favourite things. He could see at least three goat's legs pointing out of it, and the top was covered in donkey's ears!

"I even added a touch of piglet, since it's a special occasion," said Mogra, cutting him an enormous slice. Gormy clambered up a chair leg and sat down. He grabbed the cake and licked his lips. . .

GRuooOORBLE!

What was that? thought Gormy. It felt like a strange *bubbling* coming from inside him.

"Are you all right, Gormy?" asked Grumbor.

GRuooOORBLE!

There it was again, and twice as bubbling as before! It felt like Gormy's stomachs (the large one *and* the small one) were turning over and over! His head started to spin. What was going on?

"You've gone an awfully pale shade of blue," said Mogra.

Gormy felt the bubbling go all the way up his body. He felt dizzy everywhere – even in his fur! He put a paw over his mouth – but it was too late!

BUUURRRP!

It was a burp of truly epic proportions. In fact, it was so monstrous that it came out as a big, green cloud of gut-gas! It shot out of Gormy's mouth and landed on his mother's face! Mogra shrieked as the burp covered her in a cloud of green smoke and turned her whole face green.

"Eeek! I can't see!" she shrieked, as Gormy felt his stomach start to bubble again. He looked down at his blue belly, which was quivering like a bowl of badger custard. He felt the bubbling rise, and tried to clamp both hands to his mouth. . .

BuuUArrrP!

BArp! BerP!

BoRP!

BAARooP!

BuRiRUUP!

BuuUArrrP!

Bright green clouds of burp-smoke shot out of Gormy's mouth! One after the other, a barrage of belches blew across the room. And wherever they landed, a huge, green stain appeared. Grumbor took the brunt of the burps this time – on the elbow, on the ear, even one on his tail! As he dived for cover, Gormy fired another seven-and-a-half belches across the room. Within moments, the whole kitchen was filled with green smoke and covered in stains.

"What on Peatree Hill have you been eating, Gormy?" said Grumbor. "A polite burp is all very well and monstrous, but making a mess isn't!"

It couldn't be, not the fish! I ate it and everything was fine, thought Gormy. As his parents tried to catch the burps that hadn't landed yet, Gormy jumped down from the table and rushed upstairs to the bathroom. He closed the door and slumped to the floor. He had never felt so horrible!

As he lay there listening to his belly bubbling, Gormy realized something. It was such a horrible something to realize that he tried to pretend he hadn't realized it at all. But there was no escaping the truth . . . Gormy had *Croodles*.

Five

A Tale of Two Tails

"What's all the racket?"
said Mike, waking up
from a nap on the
bathroom windowsill.
"I was just waiting here
for someone to go to the loo. I'm
starving!"

"Mike! You have to help me – I have

35

Croodles!" said Gormy, as the bubbling GRuooOOORBLE! bubbled up in his belly once more! "Oh, no – here it comes again!"

But just as Gormy thought he was going to fire off another volley of brutal belches, the bubbling stopped! Gormy held his breath, waiting for something, *anything* to happen, but nothing did.

"Ha! Croodles shmoodles – see, you've beaten it already!" laughed Mike. "Croodles isn't a problem for a top-drawer monster like yourself, now is it? You swallowed that fish and you're already as right . . . as . . . rain. . ."

Mike trailed off. He was staring at Gormy, his buggy eyes even more buggy than normal.

"What? What's the matter?" Gormy asked.

"What's that behind you?" asked Mike, sounding slightly curious and fairly shocked.

"I can't see anything," said Gormy, looking around.

"No, I mean behind you . . . on your behind!"

Gormy tried to look at his bottom. He gasped in horror! He had grown an extra tail!

"AAAAAH! Get it off! Get it off!"

screamed Gormy, running around the bathroom.

"I don't know, Gormy – it looks fairly attached," said Mike, scuttying after him.

"What's happening to me?" said Gormy. He remembered what his father had said, *"Anything can happen with a bout of Croodles. . ."* Gormy started to panic. "I can't let my dad see me with an extra tail! He'll know I have Croodles! I'm just going to have to stay up here and hide . . . at least until I can get rid of my tail!"

But the next moment (as is the way with these sort of things) there was a knock at the door.

"Gormy! What's going on? Are you all right in there?" said a voice as loud as fourteen foghorns.

"It's my dad! What am I going to do?" Gormy gasped, grabbing hold of his new tail. "If Dad sees this he'll know I ate the fish!"

"Not necessarily – maybe it's just a natural part of monster-boy development," said Mike. "Do multiple tails run in your family?"

"No! I mean, I don't think so – although my Auntie Rogma does have two heads," said Gormy.

"Gormy! Open the door this instant!" yelled Grumbor. Gormy hopped on to the toilet just as his father barged into the room.

"What's going on? Why did you run off like that?" asked Grumbor.

"I just, uh, needed the loo," said Gormy, desperately trying to keep his second tail from whipping around.

"Well when you're *quite* finished, you can come downstairs and de-stain the kitchen! And don't forget your endless soap-on-a-rope!" grumbled Grumbor and then tramped off downstairs.

"How am I going to clean the kitchen without them seeing *this*?" said Gormy, holding his extra tail.

"Tuck it between your legs?" suggested Mike.

"Fat lot of help you are," sighed Gormy. He grabbed a towel and wrapped it round his waist. It stretched all the way to the floor like a long dress, covering his tails. "This will have to do until I can find a way to get rid of it," he added, and  made his way to the kitchen, making sure to pick up his endless soap-on-a-rope on the way.

Six

Blown Up

Gormy could
hardly believe the
state of the kitchen.
Huge, green burp-
stains covered the
walls, the cupboards,
even the ceiling.
Gormy felt much too

dizzy to clean, but he couldn't let on that he had Croodles. He sighed a small, sickly sigh, tied the endless soap-on-a-rope to his wrist, and got to work.

Now the good thing about endless soap-on-a-rope is that it's, well, endless. It never wears out. It's quite a remarkable creation, but particularly hard to get hold of since Grumbor ate the only wizard who made it. Still, even with a never-ending supply of soap, it was going to take a while to get the kitchen clean again.

"I want this whole place *spotless*," said his father, coming into the kitchen. "Why on Peatree Hill have you got that . . . thing wrapped around you? It looks like cloves! Are you trying to look like a hoomum?"

"No, I—" began Gormy.

"Oh, Grumbor, leave the poor boy alone.

Can't you see he's not well?" said Mogra, coming into the kitchen. Her face was still green, but she didn't seem to mind. "He's obviously caught a chill in the land beyond the hill. Fancy making him do chores when he should be curled up in front of a warm fire!"

As Grumbor grumbled suspiciously, Mogra took Gormy by the hand and led him into the sitting room. She put him on the sofa in front of the monstrously big fireplace, and stroked his head with an enormous, pink claw.

"You wait here – I'll go and smash some wood for the fire," she said, and headed for the garden. Gormy closed his eyes and breathed a sigh of relief, but as he did so he felt another GRuooOOORBLE! in his belly!

Gormy felt like he was going to burst. He held his stomach, first with one paw, then with two – then with both arms! It was then he realized that his belly was just too big to hold! He opened his eyes.

"AAaaahhh!"

He'd blown up like a balloon! And not just his belly – his whole body was inflating! He was almost three times his normal size, and completely round. He tried to stand up, but he just rolled off the sofa!

POMP!

Gormy landed on the floor, but instead of just landing, he bounced! Gormy was floating into the air! He was weightless! He bounced **POMP!** off the wall, then **POMP!** off a chair. He shrieked again as the ceiling rushed towards him. . .

P-POMP!

Gormy bounced off the ceiling, which sent him flying towards the mantelpiece!

He was heading straight for his mother's
prized collection of fine bone china bones!

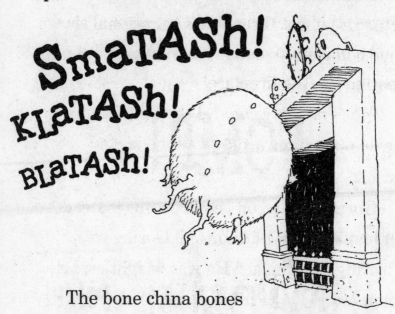

SmaTASh!
KLaTASh!
BLaTASh!

The bone china bones
smashed into a hundred-and-eleventeen
bony bits!

"Gormy! What's all that crashing?"
called Grumbor. As Gormy POMP!
POMP!POMP!-ed helplessly around the
room, he heard his father's footsteps
coming closer. He couldn't let him see him

like this. This was even worse than having an extra tail. . . Gormy looked around desperately for somewhere big enough to hide a blown-up monster boy. Finally he spotted it – the fireplace!

That's my only chance! thought Gormy. As he floated towards a wall, he kicked against it with his tiny legs and shot towards the fireplace. He closed his eyes and hoped for the best. . .

POMP!

"Gormy? Gormy Ruckles, where are you?" came his father's cry. Gormy opened his eyes. Everything was dark. He managed to turn his swollen head upwards. He could see a dot of bright light above him.

He was in the chimney!

He'd made it! He'd managed to bounce into the fireplace and up the chimney. He was safe. He was hidden.

Unfortunately, he was still floating upwards. . .

Seven

A Sticky Situation

Gormy was floating towards the top of the chimney! He'd be at the top in seconds, and then what? He'd just float off into the air – no one would ever find him! *On the plus side*, Gormy thought, *I wouldn't get into trouble. . .*

Gormy reached out with his arms to stop himself but it was no use! His head

was already out of the chimney when

BLUP!

He stopped.
Gormy was
stuck! His
body had
swollen so
much that it
was too big to fit
through the chimney.

*Well, at least I didn't float off to who
knows where*, thought Gormy. As he stared
out over Peatree Hill, he decided that, in a
competition for the weirdest thing any
monster boy had ever done, this would
probably win. He was almost at the end of
that thought when he heard the muffled
sound of his mother below.

"Where can he have got to? He was here just a minute ago. He must be delirious with fever, the poor thing's obviously caught a chill. Well, don't just stand there, Grumbor – look for him! I'll get this fire going and warm the place up for him," she said.

Gormy couldn't help but smile. His mother was convinced that he'd caught some innocent, monster cold. She was even lighting a fire to keep him warm.

Lighting a fire?!?

He was going to be cooked from below! As his mother lit the tree trunk far below him, Gormy struggled to get free – but he was stuck fast!

Before long, he felt his furry feet getting hot. Gormy panicked, wriggling and squirming with all his monstrous might!

"Put the fire out! I'm warm enough!" he cried (forgetting that he was trying to hide), but he was too far up the chimney for anyone to hear him. Then, just as he felt the tips of his two tails start to smoulder, his belly began to bubble again. **GRuooOOORBLE!**

Gormy's whole body began to shudder and shake. The pressure was building up inside him even worse than before! He felt his bottom rumble like an impatient volcano, and then

PAAAAARRRPP!

It was the most monstrously trump-tacular fart ever blown out of a bottom! Gormy shot out of the chimney like a furry, blue firework!

"AAAAaaAAAH!"

he screamed as he whizzed through the air! He whirled, spiralled and cartwheeled in every direction, propelled by violent Croodle-farts! He whooshed over the roof of the garden shed, zoomed along the surface of the lawn, and then shot up between two tallish trees. Finally, after what seemed like a lifetime of fart-induced flying, Gormy hurtled back towards the house, and straight at the bathroom window!

"Uh oh. . ." began Gormy.

SPWATP!

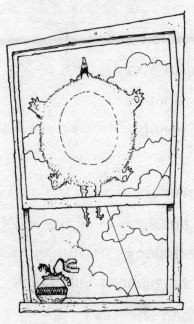

Eight

Out with the Bad

Gormy hit the window like a giant
fumblefly! His swollen body flattened
against it, and then immediately started to
slide down! As it was a very long way down
(a monster house is, of course, monstrously
large) Gormy grabbed hold of the
windowsill.

GLOooORRRtCHLE!

The bubbling was starting again! Gormy held on for dear life, but with each gut-churning rumble his grip on the windowsill got weaker. As Gormy's head spun, he felt himself slipping. . .

"Gormy, pull yourself up!" came a cry. Gormy looked up. Through the haze of dizziness he could see Mike in the bathroom! The little scuttybug pushed open the bathroom window.

With the last of his strength, Gormy pulled himself up. He squeezed through the window and dropped – **PA-DOMP!** – on to the bathroom floor.

"Blimey, what in the name of the Great Dung Heap has happened to you now?" said Mike.

"It's the Croodles! I don't know what to do, and I don't know what's going to happen next!" said Gormy. Then, as if on cue, the bubbling started again.

GLOooORRRTCHLE!

"Here it comes!" cried Gormy, flapping his arms in terror. The bubbling filled Gormy from head to toe, but it was worse than before! Then, before Mike's eyes, Gormy changed colour! First red, then green, then a sort of pale lavender, then orange! His eyes bulged out of his head and his arms spun around so quickly it looked like he might take off!

And all the time the bubbling

GUUOoOORRPLE!

got louder!

"Mike, run! It's bubbling to my bottom again!" Gormy cried. Mike dived for cover under the bathroom mat, as Gormy's bottom rumbled and thundered like an upside-down volcano. As the noise got louder and louder (and louder!) Gormy leapt on to the toilet!

SPUT-APPITY-PAPPITY-

PA-PooOOOooM!

It was a poo of truly monstrous proportions! The whole house shook!

58

Windows rattled, pictures fell off the walls (including the half-haunted portrait of Old Uncle Gobog) and the only piece of Mogra's fine bone china bone collection that wasn't broken, shattered!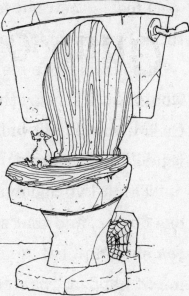

When the noise finally stopped, Mike poked his head out from under the mat, and there was Gormy, sitting on the toilet, looking exhausted.

"Gormy, you're *you* again!" said Mike. Sure enough, Gormy was no longer blown up like a balloon. Nor was he orange, red, or any shade of lavender. He'd even gone back to having just one tail!

"I feel . . . better. I feel good! Do you think I got rid of it?" puffed Gormy.

"Looks like it to me. Your dad said it would 'work its way through' in the end. Crikey, you should watch what you eat, in future – or stick to dung, like me!"

"Think I've had enough of dung for one day . . . and that's one poo that even *you* shouldn't eat. You never know what might happen," panted Gormy, staring at the impossibly monstrous poo in the toilet. He climbed up the sink to give himself a good wash (the endless soap-on-a-rope was still tied to his wrist, after all) and remove all trace of Croodles.

It was as Gormy scrubbed his left armpit that he realized something – he'd done it! He'd survived Croodles without his parents knowing he even had it! Maybe he was more monstrous than he thought!

"You know, Mike, I don't think this Croodles is all that bad! And once I flush away that Croodles-poo, my dad will never even find out that I ate the fish!" said Gormy. "Not a bad day's work, eh, Mike? Mike?"

Gormy peered over the top of the sink and looked down. Mike was nowhere to be seen – and neither was the poo! It didn't take Gormy long to realize what had happened. A sense of dread made his toeclaws tingle.

"He ate it . . . He ate the Croodles-poo!" cried Gormy, leaping out of the sink. He looked around for any sign of Mike. After a moment, he spotted something – a set of tiny, pooey footprints. *Scuttybug* footprints. Gormy followed them along the floor, then up the wall. Oddly, by the time the footprints reached the windowsill, they looked a lot bigger than the ones on the floor. What was going on? Gormy clambered up to the windowsill and stared out...

"AAAAAH!" screamed Gormy. He was met with a huge, monstrous head, at least fifty times bigger than him! It was a monster! An enormous monster – more enormous and monstrous than any monster Gormy had ever seen! It had vast, buggy eyes and long antennae, and its shell-covered head was slimy and green. In fact, when Gormy stopped screaming, the monster started to look rather familiar. A moment later Gormy realized who the monster was, and that actually, it wasn't a monster at all.

It was Mike.

Nine

Attack of the Fifty-foot Scuttybug

"*Mike?* Is that really you?" said Gormy, leaning out of the window. Mike had grown to a more-than-monstrous size! He was almost as tall as the house!

"I . . . feel . . . funny. . ." said the massively monstrous Mike in a huge, gruff voice.

"I told you not to eat the Croodles-poo!

Anything can happen! Now look at you –
you've turned into a monster Mike!" said
Gormy.

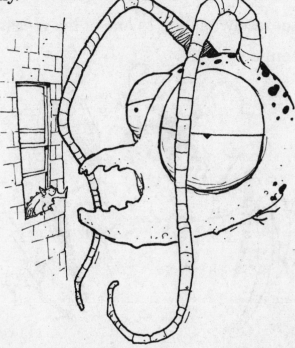

"My guts feel dizzy. . ." moaned Mike.

"You've got to hide! If my parents see
you like this they're going to realize what
happened – we've got to get you out of
here!" cried Gormy. He leapt out of the

window, on to Mike's head. "Quick, run!"

Mike began to scutty as fast as he could down the garden, as Gormy desperately held on to one of his greasy antennae.

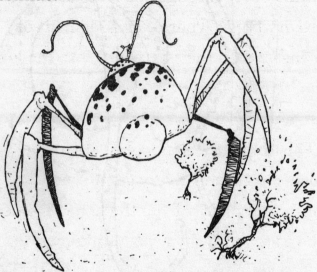

"Head for the ring of trees, we'll hide you there!" said Gormy. With Mike's new, giant legs, it took him almost no time to reach them – he was going faster than a hurried horse! Gormy shouted for Mike to stop, but he didn't. He didn't even slow down.

SCRACRAAASSH!

Mike burst through the trees as if they were dry twigs! There was a moment of darkness, then they were out, into the land beyond the hill!

Again!

This time, the land looked strangely sinister to Gormy. Every giant scutty-monster step away from the house seemed to be a step into some vast, unknown wilderness.

"Mike, stop! We have to find somewhere to hide! We're going too far away from the hill!" shouted Gormy. But by now, Mike was too full of Croodles to even know what was happening. The gigantic scuttybug

stampeded through a herd of cows, who
mooed their most terrified moos and ran in
every direction!

Then, just as Gormy wondered if Mike
was *ever* going to stop, he spotted a
hoomum village in the distance. Mike was
heading straight for it! Gormy
remembered what his father had told him

that morning, about not approaching hoomums in the day – *"If they can see you coming, they'll have time to get together and attack you."* – Well, they'd be able to see Mike coming from a mile away! The hoomums would think Mike was a monster for sure! Who knows what they'd do to him?

"Mike! Turn around!" yelled Gormy (deciding it might even be worth getting into trouble with his dad rather than take on a *whole village* of hoomums), but Mike just kept running further into the valley. Gormy crawled up Mike's head to see if he could shout into one of his ears, but he wasn't even sure where they were.

What am I going to do? Stupid Croodles! thought Gormy. Just then, he spotted the endless soap-on-a-rope, still

tied to his wrist. He immediately had an idea. *If the endless soap-on-a-rope can clean the Croodle-burps, maybe it can clean Mike!* he thought. It was his only chance to save his friend. Gormy took the endless soap-on-a-rope off his wrist, then began climbing up one of Mike's long antennae. It shook as Mike ran, but Gormy kept climbing, pulling himself along until he reached the end. Gormy stared ahead – they were almost at the hoomum village!

Suddenly, Gormy slipped! He held on with one paw as he dangled on the antenna, face to face with the monstrously massive Mike. The scuttybug's eyes were glazed over, and his mouth was wide open as he belched and burped. Gormy had a clear shot. He held on tight, and took aim. . .

"Hey Mike – eat this!" he cried, and threw the soap!

It landed in Mike's mouth and disappeared into his belly! Gormy tried to hold on, but he was still slipping. . . If the hoomums didn't get him, he was going to be trampled by his best friend!

Just then, Mike's expression changed. He started to shake from side to side, and bright pink steam shot out of his body in every direction! Then, as the steam poured into the air, Mike began to get smaller. He went from being as big as twenty cows, to ten, to one!

Gormy could barely see through the clouds of steam – he had no idea what was happening until he suddenly felt the touch of grass beneath his feet! He let go of Mike's antenna, and rolled

GIOMP! GOMP! GUMP!

along the ground! It should have hurt but after a bout of Croodles, Gormy barely noticed a few scuffs and bruises. He scrambled to his feet. In the distance, he could see the hoomums pouring out of their houses and grouping together. They must have seen Mike! They were coming to get him!

"Mike? Mike, where are you?" said Gormy. After a moment, he heard a tiny, gruff voice.

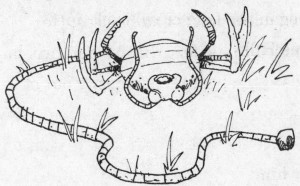

"Oi, watch where you're standing – you nearly squashed me flat!"

"Mike, you're *you* again!" cried Gormy, looking down. Sure enough, there was Mike, back to normal and flat on his back. Next to him was a small piece of rope, but the soap had completely disappeared.

"Not so endless, after all," said Gormy. He scooped Mike up and popped him on his shoulder.

"What happened?" asked Mike. "I hardly remember anything after eating that tasty bit of dung."

"I'll tell you all about it later, Mike," said Gormy. He stared back at the hoomums. Since Mike was small again, they could no longer see him, so they just ran about and shouted like headless Hop-gobbins. Gormy ducked down in the long grass before they noticed him, and began the long crawl back up Peatree Hill.

Ten

A Perfectly Monstrous Birthday

It took Gormy and Mike quite some time
to get back to the house. So long, in fact,
that by the time they walked through the
back door it was starting to get dark.
Needless to say, Gormy's parents had
noticed he was missing. They were
waiting for him in the kitchen.

"Gormy! Where have you been? Don't

you know what time it is? Have you seen the state of my bone china bones? What has got into you today?" Mogra said in one breath.

"No more nonsense, Gormy," said Grumbor, sternly. "You're going to tell us what's been going on, and I want the *truth*."

Gormy thought about thinking up a lie – he even looked for Mike to see if he had any ideas, but he'd already scuttied off. In the end, the only thing that he could think of to say was "Croodles".

Grumbor almost fell over at the mention of the word. Gormy confessed everything – eating the fish, the bubbling, the burps and the breakages – even the whole giant, monstrous scuttybug thing, which sounded like a lie, but wasn't. After he had finished, there was a very long silence.

"So you mean to tell me that you disobeyed me?" said Grumbor.

"Y-yes," muttered Gormy, his pointy blue ears drooping.

"And you mean to say that you ate a fish, got a bad case of Croodles, burped all over the kitchen, grew an extra tail, blew up like a balloon, got fired out the chimney, flew around the garden, *and* rode a giant scuttybug into the land beyond the hill?" continued Grumbor.

"Um, yes. . ." whimpered Gormy. He held his breath and waited for the shouting to start . . . but it never did.

"Well, that sounds like a perfectly monstrous birthday to me, wouldn't you say, Mogra?" said Grumbor, grinning from tusk to tusk.

"I couldn't agree more – what a monstrous way to celebrate turning one-eighth-and-an-eighth!" laughed Mogra.

Gormy couldn't believe it!

"So, you're not angry?" he asked, scratching his furry blue head.

"Why would we be angry? That was a

very monstrous thing you did, dealing with Croodles all on your own," said Grumbor. Then he leaned down to Gormy and whispered in his ear: "You know, the truth is, I've never actually *had* Croodles. I had the fish in my hands, but when my father told me about Croodles, I didn't dare eat it!"

"You mean, you made it up?" said Gormy, more bewildered than he had ever been.

"I think you'll be quite the monster when you're older," said Mogra. "But there's plenty of time for that! Now, who's for birthday cake?"

Eleven

Lesson Six Hundred and Eleventy-seven
Monsters can't Eat Fish

After tucking into a few slices of cake (and a whole goat's leg), Gormy realized how tired he was. Everyone agreed that the tidying up could wait until tomorrow, so Gormy made his way up to his room. He was about to get into bed when he spotted his **How to be a Better Monster** book. He opened it up at the first blank page and stared at it. Even though he wasn't a proper monster yet, Gormy had been pretty monstrous! He'd survived Croodles – and even his father hadn't done that!

Gormy took an angry bee out of his bee jar, and wrote:

LESSON SIX HUNDRED AND ELEVENTY-SEVEN:

MONSTERS CAN'T EAT FISH

Then he thought for a moment and added:

UNLESS THEY'RE <u>REALLY</u> MONSTROUS

I can't wait for my next birthday, thought Gormy. He swallowed the bee, and climbed into bed. He fell straight into a

deep sleep, and dreamed of monstrous
things – roaring, stomping, smashing . . .
and fishing!

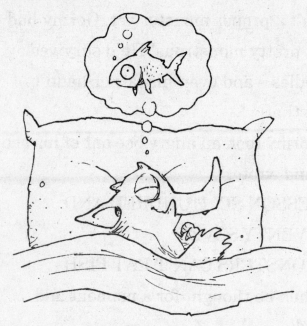

GORMY RUCKLES
MONSTER BOY

MONSTER laughs!

GUY BASS
Illustrations by Ross Collins

GORMY RUCKLES
MONSTER Mischief

GUY BASS

Illustrations by Ross Collins

MONSTER laughs!

Meet Charlie – he's trouble!

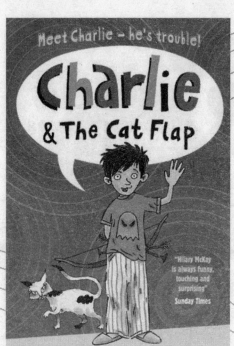

Meet Charlie – he's trouble!

Charlie and Henry are staying the
night at Charlie's house. They've made
a deal, but the night doesn't go quite
as Charlie plans. . .

Meet Charlie – he's trouble!

Charlie's fed up with his mean family always picking on him – so he's decided to run away. That'll show them! Now they'll be sorry!

But running away means being boringly, IMPOSSIBLY quiet…

Meet Charlie – he's trouble!

"The snow's all getting wasted! What'll we do? It will never last till after school!"

Charlie's been waiting for snow his whole life, but now it's come, everyone's trying to spoil it! Luckily, Charlie has a very clever plan to keep it safe…

Meet Charlie – he's trouble!

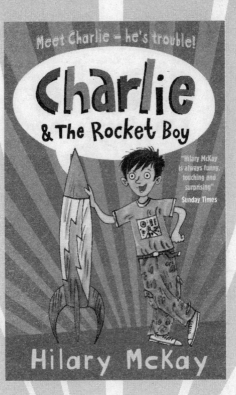

Meet Charlie – he's trouble!

Charlie
& The Rocket Boy

"Hilary McKay
is always funny,
touching and
surprising"
Sunday Times

Hilary McKay

*"Zachary is a liar, liar,
pants on fire!"*

There's a new boy in Charlie's class. Zachary
says his dad is away on a rocket but Charlie
knows that's rubbish… Isn't it?

Meet Charlie – he's trouble!

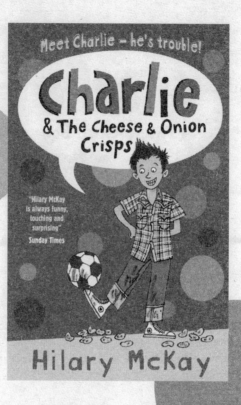

Meet Charlie – he's trouble!

Charlie
& The Cheese & Onion Crisps

"Hilary McKay is always funny, touching and surprising"
Sunday Times

Hilary McKay

*Charlie has given up
cheese and onion crisps!*

He just hasn't been himself lately.
There's only one thing for it – the
Truly Amazing Smarties Trick!